Victoria Turnbull

Pandora

Frances Lincoln
Children's Books

Pandora lived alone,

in a land of broken things.

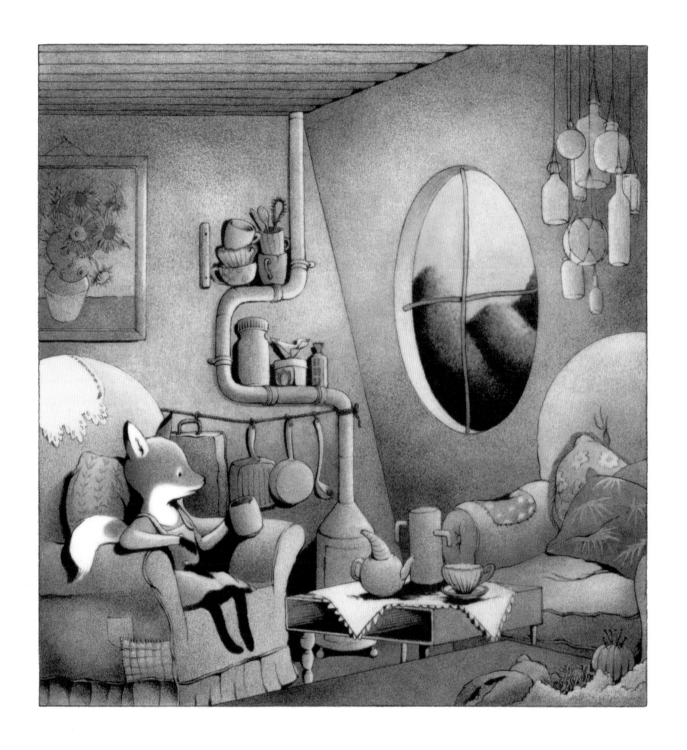

She made herself a handsome home, from all that people had left behind.

But no one ever came to visit.

So she spent her time gathering and repairing what she could,
bringing lost and forgotten things back to life.

Then one day...

... something fell from the sky.

It was broken too,

but Pandora didn't know how to fix it.

So she made it as snug as she could
and kept it safe all through the night.

Pandora's guest was a little weak at first.

But as the days went by, he grew stronger.

Soon he could hop about,
and then fly short distances.

Before long, Pandora couldn't keep up with him.

But, with gifts from
faraway lands,

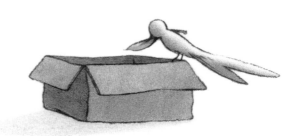

he always came back.

Until the day he didn't.

Once again, Pandora was alone.

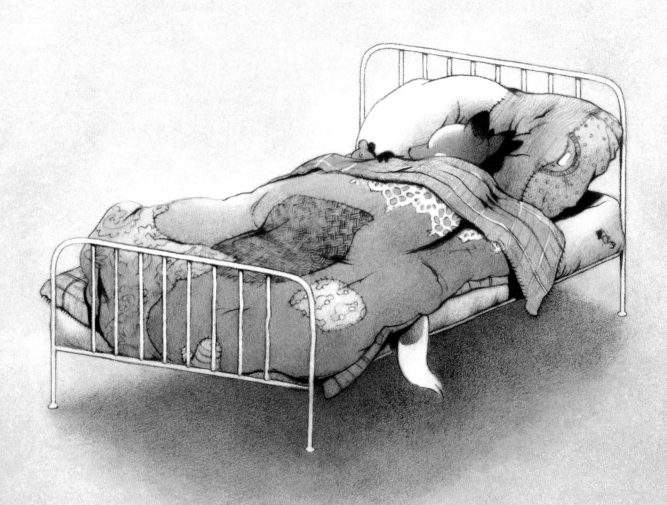

She thought her heart would break.

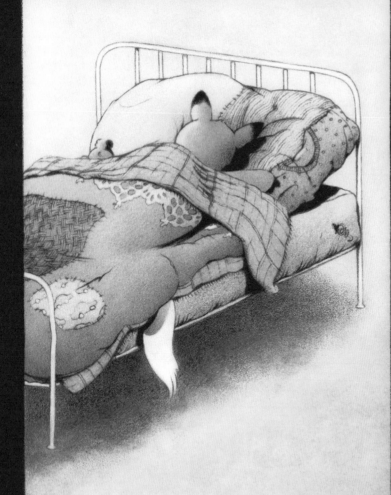

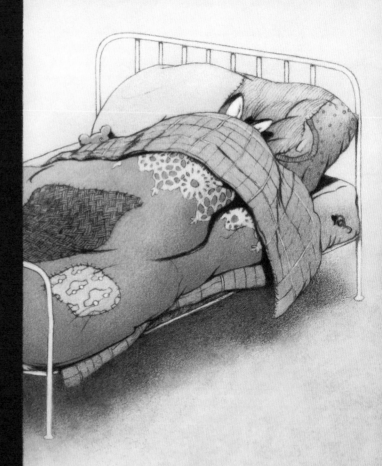

But day by day,

the world appeared

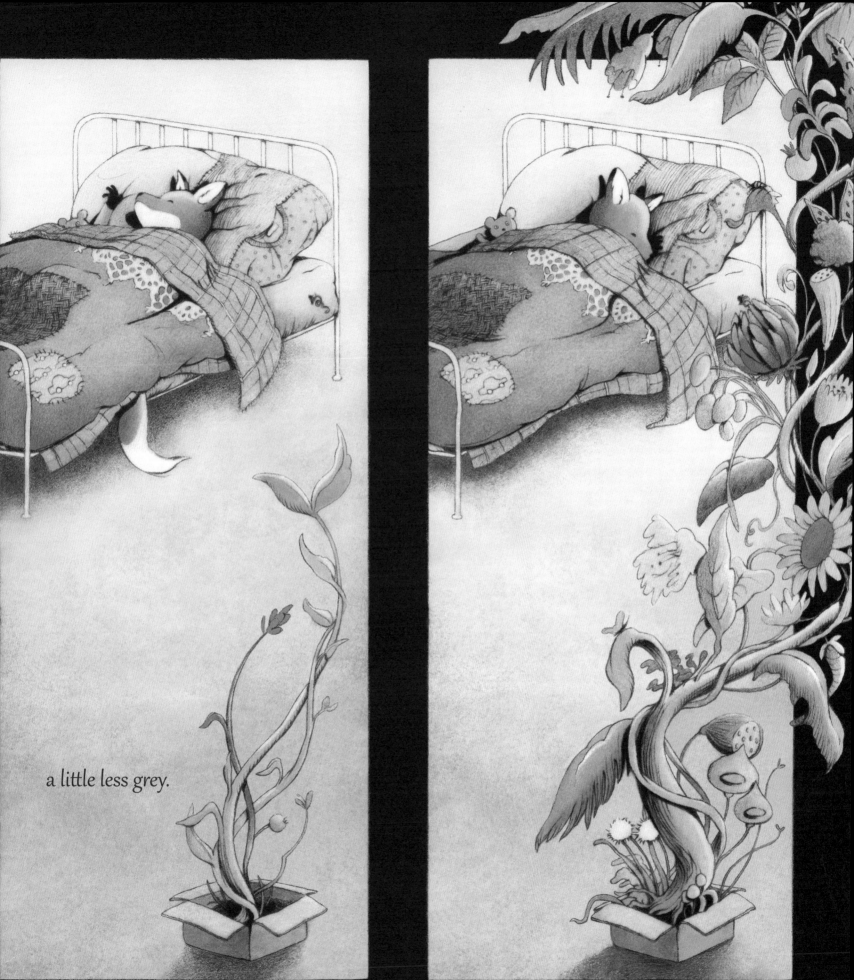

a little less grey.

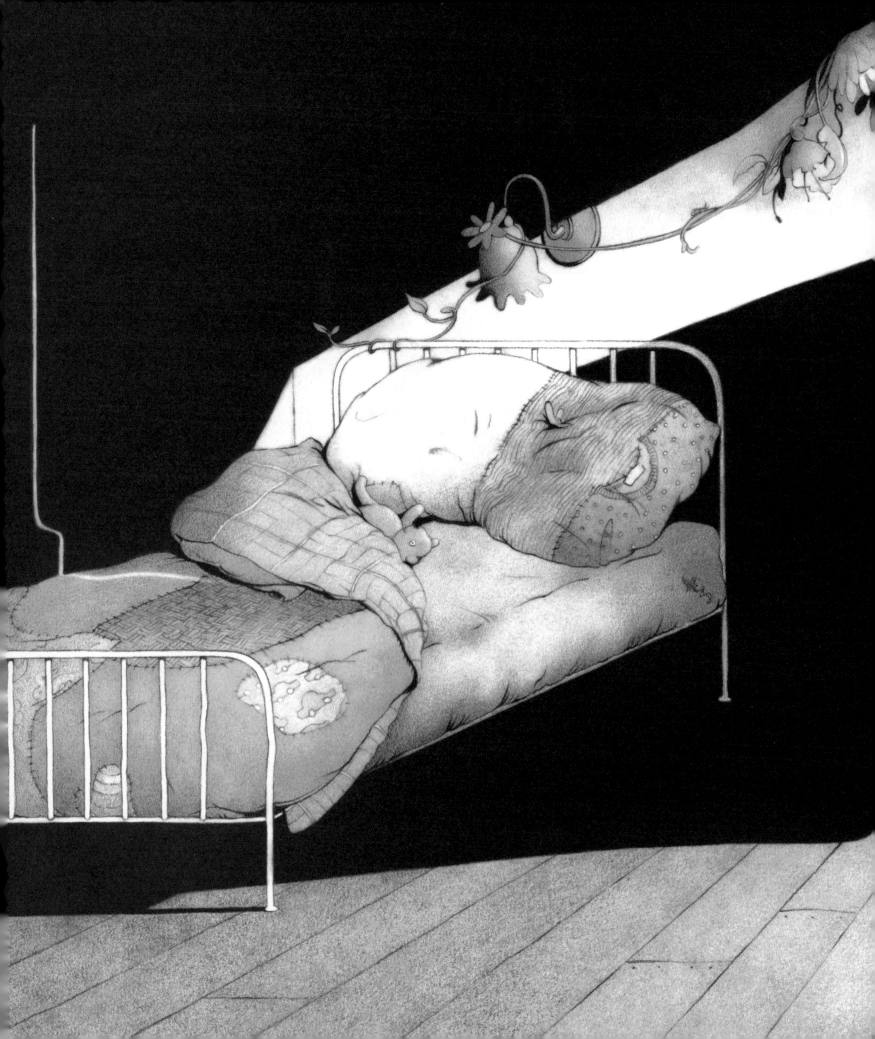

Until one morning, Pandora woke
to the warmth of the sun...

and to the sound of birdsong...

in a land of living things.

For Mum & Dad.

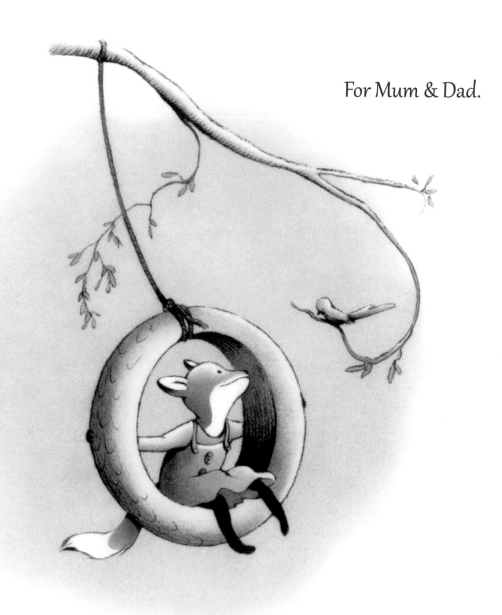

First published in 2016 by Frances Lincoln Children's Books,
74-77 White Lion Street, London N1 9PF
QuartoKnows.com
Visit out blogs at QuartoKnows.com

Text and illustrations copyright © Victoria Turnbull 2016

A catalogue record for this book is available from the British Library

ISBN 978-1-84780-749-6

Edited by Katie Cotton
Published by Rachel Williams · Production by Laura Grandi

Illustrated with graphite and coloured pencil
Set in Gabriola

Printed in China

1 3 5 7 9 8 6 4 2